FLAT STANLEY

Goes Camping

EGMONT

We bring stories to life

Book Band: Turquoise

First published in Great Britain 2013
This Reading Ladder edition published 2016
by Egmont UK Limited
The Yellow Building, 1 Nicholas Road, London W11 4AN
Text copyright © 2013 and illustrations copyright © 2014 by the Trust u/w/o Richard C. Brown
a/k/a Jeff Brown f/b/o Duncan Brown
Illustrations by Jon Mitchell
The author and illustrator have asserted their moral rights
ISBN 978 1 4052 8208 6
www.egmont.co.uk
A CIP catalogue record for this title is available from the British Library.
Printed in Singapore
47002/3

Series consultant: Nikki Gamble

FLAT STANLEY

Goes Camping

Written by Lori Haskins Houran   Illustrations by Jon Mitchell

Based on the original character created by Jeff Brown

Reading Ladder

Stanley Lambchop lived with his mother, his father, and his little brother, Arthur.

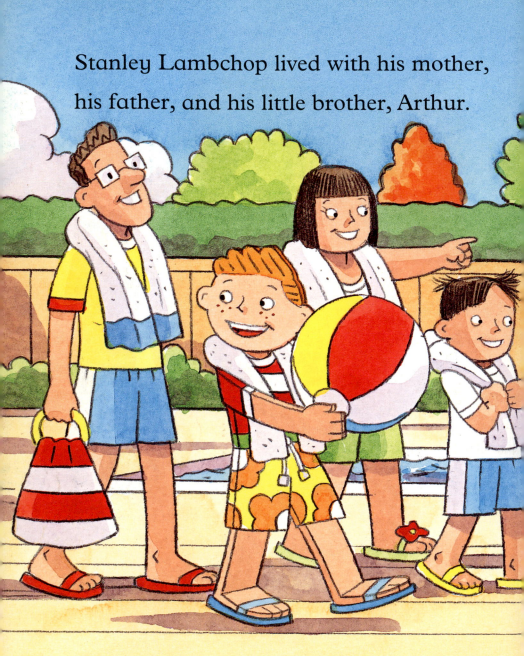

Stanley was four feet tall, about a foot wide, and half an inch thick. He had been flat ever since a bulletin board fell on him.

There were lots of good things about being flat.

Stanley could put on suncream in one swipe.

Stanley had the best back float at the pool.

Stanley had the loudest belly flop, too.

But sometimes it was hard
being the only flat kid in town.

'I'm sick of being flat,'
said Stanley one morning.
'Flat is lame.'

'Lame?' said Mrs Lambchop. 'Why, some of the best things in the world are flat!'

'Like the newspaper,'
said Mr Lambchop.

'And fried eggs. And pancakes. And bacon,' said Arthur.

'I guess so,' said Stanley.

After breakfast Mr Lambchop
started loading up the car
with tents and sleeping bags.

'What's going on?' asked Arthur.

'We're going camping.' said
Mrs Lambchop. 'This
family needs some fresh air.'

'All right!' yelled Arthur.
Stanley barely smiled.

After a short drive, the Lambchops
arrived at the Roarin' River
Campground.
Stanley was helpful, as usual.
He helped carry firewood.

ROARIN'
RIVER
CAMPGROUND

Stanley blocked the wind

so his mother could start a fire.

But Stanley just wasn't himself.

He wouldn't even eat any toast.

'Why don't you two go exploring?' suggested Mr Lambchop.

'Good idea,' said Mrs Lambchop.

'Just don't get lost . . .

. . . or fall off a cliff . . .

. . . or touch any poison ivy.

Have fun, dears!'

Stanley and Arthur set out.

'Hey, animal tracks!' said Arthur.

'Let's follow them!'

The boys followed the tracks
along the river, through some trees,
and up a steep hill
with a cliff on one side.

'The tracks end here,' said Arthur.

He peered over the cliff.

'I wonder what kind of animal

made them.'

'Um, Arthur,' said Stanley.

Arthur turned around.

'Skunk!' Stanley whispered.

'Let's get out of here!'

But the boys were trapped.

The skunk was on one side.

The cliff was on the other.

Then the skunk raised its tail!

'What do we do?' Arthur wailed.

'Mum said not to fall off a cliff,' said Stanley. 'She didn't say not to jump off.'

Suddenly Stanley grabbed Arthur by both hands and jumped!

'AAAAAAAAAAAAHHHHH!'
Arthur screamed.

Then Arthur opened his eyes.

He wasn't falling.

He was sailing!

32

Above him, Stanley's body
made the perfect parachute.

33

The boys landed with a gentle PLOP.

'That was awesome!' said Arthur.

'Thanks,' said Stanley.

'Now, where are we?'

Arthur and Stanley looked around.

All they saw were trees.

BEWARE
OF
POISON
IVY

'We're lost!' said Arthur.

'And it's getting dark!'

Then Stanley spotted something.

'There's the river!' he said.

'Our campground is on the river!'

The boys ran to the water's edge.

About a mile downstream

were two cozy Lambchop tents!

'What can we do?
It will be dark before we
can walk that far,'
said Arthur.

'I know!' said Stanley.

Stanley got a running start
and belly flopped into the river.

SPLASH!

Then he flipped over on to his back.

'Climb on!'

'Woohoo!' cried Arthur.

'I always wanted to go rafting!'

Arthur and Stanley made it
back to camp, drippy but safe.
'Let's keep this to ourselves,'
said Stanley.

'I can't believe we got lost

AND went off a cliff,' Arthur said.

'At least we didn't touch poison ivy!'

'There you are!' said Mrs Lambchop.
'Just in time for supper.'

That night, Arthur whispered
to Stanley from his sleeping bag,
'You know, if you weren't flat,
you couldn't have saved us today.'

Stanley smiled. 'Maybe being flat isn't so lame,' he said.

And the next day, Stanley found out another good thing about being flat.

He could put on poison ivy cream
in one swipe.